A SPECIAL TRICK

STORY AND PICTURES BY

MERCER MAYER

The Dial Press, New York

Copyright © 1970 by Mercer Mayer
All rights reserved.
Library of Congress catalog card number: 69-18220
Printed in the United States of America
First Pied Piper Printing
ISBN 0-8037-8103-2

"Will you show me that trick again, please?" asked Elroy as the magician bowed at the end of his performance.

"No, my little friend. A true magician never does the same trick twice in one day, for if he does, his magic will soon wear out."

"If I work for you, will you show me some tricks?" Elroy asked.

"I'll tell you what," said the magician. "Every day after a performance you may sweep the stage and dust. Then I will do a special trick just for you. But you must be careful not to touch anything on the table. Some of the boxes, hats, and vases have very strong magic powers, and it would be unwise for you to let these powers loose."

· 3 ·

"Oh, I will be very careful. I promise."
Elroy answered.

"I have to go to a very important magicians'
conference now. I hope to be back by tomorrow
morning." The magician handed Elroy the
broom and left.

Elroy swept the floor and dusted here and
there, being very careful not to touch anything
on the table. Every so often he saw a spooky
glow come from one of the vases or some mist
rise from a hat. And once or twice Elroy even
thought he heard whispering voices coming
from one of the shiny boxes.

As he was sweeping the floor, Elroy noticed
something lying in a corner. When he walked
closer, he discovered that it was a very old book
covered in crusty leather. Elroy picked it up
and thought to himself, I bet this book fell off

the table. The magician will probably be upset if he sees it on the floor, so I'd better put it back. As he lay the crusty old book on the table, it fell open and Elroy saw very strange words written all over the page.

Elroy took a closer look. He read to himself: *To call a galaplop, say Bing-dong-galaplop-bee-there.* Why this is a magician's dictionary, Elroy thought. But what do the words stand for? "I wonder what Bing-dong-galaplop-bee-there means," said Elroy to no one in particular. "And what's a galaplop anyway?"

"I'm a galaplop," thundered a loud voice in Elroy's ears. With a creak and a moan the ground yawned open. Billows of green smoke poured into the air and a very large shape rose out of the hole behind him. Turning around, Elroy saw six eyes peering at him.

"I knew that someday that book would fall into the hands of a fool," the galaplop said with a wicked laugh.

Elroy clutched the book and tried to get out of the way. Instead he backed into the table. Jars, boxes, hats, and vases spilled all over the

stage. He remembered the magician's warning. Now I've done it, he thought. A gigantic slithering shape with two red eyes as big as watermelons oozed into the air from the largest of the vases. With the most horrible howl Elroy had ever heard, it lunged at the galaplop.

"I've waited hundreds of years to get you, Galaplop, and now's my chance."

The six-eyed galaplop roared and the watermelon-eyed monster howled. They fought and thrashed around. The tent thrashed around too.

"Help! Stop it! The magician will be furious," Elroy called. The monsters went on fighting. He started thumbing wildly through the old book. Maybe he could find a spell that would fix things. In his panic Elroy yelled out the first words he saw. "Airis fare o farethee air. Fillthee air with hoppen hare." Suddenly the tent was filled with hopping rabbits the size of big pigs.

His eyes searching the pages, Elroy then said,

"Iga jig—take a swig. Fillthee air with noiseepig."
Immediately after he said the words, Elroy knew he had made a big mistake. Squealing pigs the size of rabbits began to romp with rabbits the size of pigs. The many-eyed monsters fought on.

"What am I going to do?" moaned Elroy.

After searching and searching, flipping page after page, going down column after column, Elroy finally saw what he was looking for. *To clear up an unpleasant situation, say Sprittle sprattle nattle tattle.* And just for good measure he added a phrase that happened to catch his eye. All together Elroy said, "Sprittle sprattle nattle tattle, gone is thee gloomy room."

The pigs, the rabbits, the two fighting monsters, and the tent melted away right in front of his eyes. Elroy found himself sitting on the ground under the stars, still holding tightly to the magic book.

"Oh, no! Where are my trousers?" Elroy cried. His trousers were gone, along with everything else. Since he hadn't let his mother wash them in such a long time, they too had become an unpleasant situation.

"What a mess. The magician will really be angry with me if he can't find his tent when he comes back. And my mother will be angry if I'm not home soon." So Elroy trudged off with the crusty old book under his arm and his underpants peeking out from under his jacket.

He figured it would be best to go right up to his room. His mother thought he was sick and wanted to give him some medicine. "Oh, I'm not that sick, Mom, I'm just a little sick. And besides I'm going straight to bed," said Elroy as he shut the door. After his mother had come up to wish him pleasant dreams, he lit a small candle and began to read through the magic book, making very sure not to utter one word out loud. The book was very thick and had magical sayings in it for every occasion. There was a saying that would turn roses into toads. There was a saying that would turn a bed into a pony with wings. Elroy thought that one might come in handy so he said it to himself silently three times in order to memorize it:

Ding bag wing-ed nag.

Ding bag wing-ed nag.

Ding bag wing-ed nag.

Elroy was the fastest reader in his class in school, but by two o'clock in the morning he was only halfway through the book. By the time he had reached the last paragraph of the last page, the sun was shining through his window. Then he read the last sentence. *To reverse all spells one*

at a time, shout as loudly as you can: Ding bog farthum still. And if that doesn't work, shout it

backward: Still farthum bog ding. "I finally found it!" he shouted.

Then he remembered. "Ding bag wing-ed nag," he called, and his bed turned into a pony with wings. Elroy picked up the book from the floor, jumped onto the pony's back, and flew out the window, straight across town and right to the spot where the magician's tent had been.

Getting off the pony, Elroy shouted, "Ding bog farthum still," and made it disappear. He hoped it was back in his bedroom in the shape of a bed.

Again Elroy shouted, "Ding bog farthum still." A mist fell from the air and covered the ground all around him. Slowly the tent took shape overhead. Elroy heard the roaring sounds of the two monsters fighting and watched as they began to appear through the mist, fighting and thrashing around. The hopping rabbits that were the size of big pigs and the squealing pigs that were the size of rabbits were there too, running and jumping and even flying all over the place. As if this was not enough, the tent had a big hole in the top and the canvas was flapping loudly.

"Ding bog farthum still," Elroy shouted and the squealing pigs disappeared. "Ding bog

farthum still," he shouted again and the hopping rabbits disappeared. "Ding bog farthum still," he shouted for the third time and waited for the monsters to disappear. But they were making so much noise that they didn't even hear him. He remembered that if the spell

didn't work, it could be shouted backward.
"Still farthum bog ding." The two monsters
looked at Elroy and growled, but Elroy was not
frightened. He knew by now that the spell
could not be ignored. "Ding bog farthum still—   · 23
still farthum bog ding," he shouted just to make

sure there were no mistakes. The monsters finally obeyed: The galaplop sank back into his hole in the ground, which rumbled shut, and the watermelon-eyed monster slithered back into the overturned vase.

Now that he had some peace and quiet, Elroy took a good look around him. Everything was a mess. Stage props were knocked over, curtains were pulled down, the table was overturned, and boxes, hats, and vases were scattered all over the place.

He quickly set up the table and began putting everything back. Every once in a while when he picked up a vase, it would rumble and one of the boxes even began to open. But Elroy just said,

· 24 ·

"Ding bog farthum still," and everything was quiet. Suddenly a creepy crawly thing poked its head out of a magician's hat and handed Elroy his trousers. Elroy smiled and said, "Thank you very much. Ding bog farthum still." With a cry of protest the creepy crawly thing disappeared back into the hat.

Elroy put on his trousers, and when he was finished cleaning, looked around and wondered what he could do about the hole in the top of the tent. Looking under *T* in the index of the book, Elroy found:

Tent: To create a tent out of a camel . . . "No, that's not what I want."

To make a purple tent . . . "No, not that either."

To have a larger tent . . . "No."

To have a smaller tent . . . "No, no, no."

To mend a hole in a tent—"Yes, that's it," Elroy shouted—*say Hoodunit-notmee.*

"Hoodunit-notmee," said Elroy, and the hole disappeared.

He looked around one last time just to make sure everything was in place and then sat down to rest. Just before he closed his eyes, he looked up and saw another hole—a smaller one in the side of the tent. But Elroy was too tired to cast any more spells. Soon he was fast asleep.

The next thing he heard was the magician's loud voice. "Wake up, wake up, my little friend. You must have fallen asleep. And how nicely you've cleaned up everything."

Elroy awoke with a start and struggled to his feet. "Oh, thank you, sir, but I must go home. The sun is up and my mother will worry."

"Oh, but you mustn't go before I do a special trick for you as my part of our bargain." The magician pulled a lollipop out of Elroy's ear and handed it to him.

"Thank you, sir, for the wonderful, special trick." Elroy tried not to laugh. Boy, could I show you a thing or two, he thought. "I'd better be going before my mom and dad wake up." Waving good-bye to the magician, he ran home and crawled into bed before anyone in the house was up.

Just before falling asleep, Elroy muttered under his breath, "Ding bag wing-ed nag," and

his bed turned into a pony with wings. "Ding bog farthum still," he muttered, and the pony turned back into his bed.

I knew it wasn't a dream, Elroy thought, and fell asleep.